William Shakespeare

Macbeth

Retold by
Marcia Williams

WALKER
BOOKS

Contents

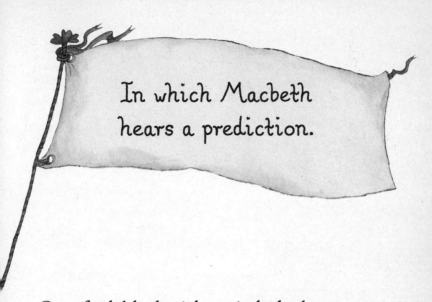

In which Macbeth
hears a prediction.

On a foul, bleak night, rain lashed across
the Scottish heath, and through the roaring
thunder and cracking lightning came an
unearthly cry: "When shall we three meet
again? In thunder, lightning, or in rain?"

"When the hurlyburly's done," came the answer. "When the battle's lost and won."

"Where the place?"

"Upon the heath."

"There to meet with Macbeth," said a third voice.

The following morning, the beating of a drum could be heard across the same bleak landscape. Closer and closer it came to the place where the unearthly cries had been heard. The drum beat heralded Macbeth and Banquo, two Scottish generals returning home to Inverness.

They had just defeated an army of rebels who had risen against Macbeth's cousin, King Duncan. Few had ever seen such courage as the two generals had shown in the battle. It was said that Macbeth had brandished his sword with such speed that it smoked with the blood of his enemies. Certainly, both men were so stained with blood that even the pouring rain could not remove it.

"So foul and fair a day I have not seen," shouted Macbeth against the storm.

Suddenly, as if from nowhere, three weird creatures rose out of the gloom. Both men stopped in their tracks.

"What are these, so wither'd and so wild in their attire?" gasped Banquo.

The creatures seemed to be women, but they had beards. Were they real or were the generals imagining them?

"Are you aught that man may question?" asked Banquo. He had heard that there were witches living on the heath who could tell you your future.

The three witches, if that is what they were, put their bony fingers to their skinny lips as if to silence Banquo. They turned to Macbeth.

"All hail, Macbeth," cried the first. "Hail to thee, Thane of Glamis!"

Macbeth was taken aback – the first witch had addressed him correctly, but how did she know who he was?

"All hail, Macbeth! Hail to thee, Thane of Cawdor!" said the second, which was strange, as he was not the Thane of Cawdor.

Strangest of all was the third witch's greeting: "All hail, Macbeth, thou shall be king hereafter!"

Maybe these were more than greetings – maybe these were prophecies. Banquo was excited at the possibility, and asked

the witches to look into the seeds of time and say what his future held.

"Thou shalt get kings, though thou be none:

so, all hail, Macbeth and Banquo!" said the witches. With that, they disappeared like bubbles into the chilly air.

"Whither are they vanish'd?" asked Banquo, amazed.

Macbeth gave no answer, for already his mind was consumed with the idea that he might one day be King of Scotland!

Moments later news arrived, sent from King Duncan. The king had made Macbeth Thane of Cawdor in honour of his great

victory. The two generals stood stunned –
the witches' first prediction had come true
already!

Macbeth turned to Banquo. "Do you not
hope your children shall be kings, when
those that gave the Thane of Cawdor to me
promised no less to them?" he asked.

Banquo smiled at his friend. He was more
cautious than Macbeth and less swayed by
ambition, and he warned Macbeth that such
creatures of the dark might have evil intent.
They could be trying to trick Macbeth
into some deed that would have dire
consequences. But Macbeth brushed away
the warning.

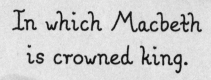

In which Macbeth is crowned king.

In the days that followed, Macbeth could think of nothing but the crown – the crown of Scotland that would sit on his head when he was the king! How soon would that be, he wondered. Should he be doing something to make sure it happened? No, he thought to himself. "If chance will have me king, why, chance may crown me, without my stir." But the seed of ambition had been sown by the three witches, and ambition is an evil master. Dark thoughts began to stir in Macbeth's mind – thoughts of ways he could hasten the day of his coronation.

When Banquo and Macbeth finally arrived at the palace, King Duncan could not have greeted them more warmly or with more gratitude for their great bravery.

"O worthiest cousin! Welcome hither!" he cried. "I have begun to plant thee, and will labour to make thee full of growing. Noble Banquo, that hast no less deserved, let me infold thee and hold thee to my heart."

Such a greeting from the king would have swelled the hearts of most men, but not Macbeth's. For shortly afterwards, King Duncan named his son, Malcolm, heir to the throne of Scotland. This was the honour that Macbeth had been hoping to receive.

"Stars, hide your fires!" Macbeth muttered to himself. "Let not light see my black and deep desires."

King Duncan went on to say that he would visit Macbeth's castle at Inverness. Again, Macbeth should have been pleased by this honour. But now he was consumed by the desire to be king and all he could think about was that Malcolm now stood in his way. Maybe he could not rely on chance to make him king ... maybe he would have to give chance a helping hand!

Macbeth couldn't wait to tell his wife all that had happened, so he sent a letter ahead to her. Her excitement grew as she read it,

for she was even greedier for power than
Macbeth. She could already see the golden
crown of Scotland on her husband's head.
Macbeth was ambitious, but he had a sense
of honour. Lady Macbeth was quite ruthless
and only honoured power and ambition. She
was capable of destroying anyone who stood
in her husband's way.

By the time Macbeth reached his castle,
Lady Macbeth was already plotting
King Duncan's death! When she greeted

Macbeth she saw that his thoughts had also
turned to murder, but she was worried by
his lack of cunning. "Your face, my thane,
is as a book where men may read strange

matters," she warned him. "Look like the innocent flower, but be the serpent under't."

Their talk was interrupted by the arrival of King Duncan and his two sons, Prince Malcolm and Prince Donalbain. The king was delighted by the sweet air around the castle, and by Lady Macbeth, who appeared so charming and welcoming. But Lady Macbeth was secretly urging her husband to kill him that night.

In preparation for the evil deed, Lady Macbeth drugged King Duncan's two guards, who lay beside the king as he slept.

Now that murder had become a reality, Macbeth was agonizing over it. King Duncan was a good and gentle man, and a guest in Macbeth's house. It was his duty to protect the king, not to murder him.

"We will proceed no further in this business," he told his wife. "If we should fail?"

"Screw your courage to the sticking-place and we'll not fail!" Lady Macbeth scorned.

So, swayed by his wife, Macbeth

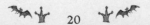

reluctantly agreed to murder the king as he lay in bed that night. Lady Macbeth's evil heart swelled with satisfaction and she retired to her chamber to await the time.

Macbeth remained hunched in his chair, imagining the fearful deed that lay before him. His dark thoughts were interrupted by the arrival of Banquo and his son Fleance. Banquo had brought a gift from the king: a beautiful diamond for Lady Macbeth, whom King Duncan had called his "most kind hostess"! Macbeth inwardly groaned. Could he really murder this man, this king, this giver of gifts and sweet compliments?

"I dreamt last night of the three weird sisters," said Banquo. "To you they have show'd some truth."

"I think not of them," lied Macbeth, trying to end the conversation.

When Banquo left him, he dismissed the last of the servants and tried to prepare himself for the foul murder. He paced up and down the great hall, trying to gather courage, but then he saw a phantom dagger hovering in front of him. "Is this a dagger  which I see before me, the handle toward my hand?" he cried.

Meanwhile, Lady Macbeth, fearing her husband's courage would fail him, had decided she would have to murder King Duncan herself.

She crept into his
room and looked
upon the sleeping
guards. "That which
hath made them

drunk hath made me bold!" she whispered.

Satisfied that they would not wake, she took their daggers and raised them above the king. But just as she was about to plunge the daggers downwards she looked at his face and froze. King Duncan looked so like her own father that she felt her courage leave her.

She dropped the
daggers and fled
from the room,
shaken by her
failure.

Lady Macbeth ran to find her husband, for time was running out and the guards would soon wake from their stupor. She waited outside while Macbeth crept into King Duncan's room.

Reluctantly, Macbeth picked up the daggers. Closing his eyes, he plunged them into King Duncan's heart. Then he ran from the room, his hands dark with the king's

blood and the daggers still clenched in his fists.

"I have done the deed," he cried,

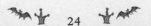

overwhelmed with the horror of it.

"Why did you bring these daggers from the place?" cried Lady Macbeth. "They must lie there: go carry them, and smear the sleepy grooms with blood."

Macbeth would not go back – he was too afraid to see what he had done.

"Infirm of purpose!" cried Lady Macbeth furiously. "Give me the daggers!"

She grabbed the daggers and ran to return them to the grooms, covering their hands and faces with blood for good measure.

Later, when King Duncan's body was found, the whole castle rocked with cries of "murder and treason"! For he was the most noble of sovereigns and was loved by all.

Macbeth's guilt made him feel that all eyes were upon him. He was terrified of being discovered so, claiming vengeance, he killed both the guards before they could be questioned and reveal their innocence. "O! Yet I do repent me of my fury, that I did kill them," he said.

Despite his display of grief, many suspected that Macbeth, aided by his wife, had murdered the king. The king's two sons

feared for their own lives and decided to flee from Scotland, Malcolm to England and Donalbain to Ireland. So Macbeth, as next in line to the throne, was crowned King of Scotland. He had achieved his

ambition and had also fulfilled the witches'
third prophecy.

"Thou hast it now: king, Cawdor, Glamis,
all, as the weird women promised," Banquo
said to himself, "and I fear thou play'dst most
foully for't."

Macbeth
was haunted
by the fear
of being
discovered,
as well as his

own guilt. He worried that Banquo would
find proof of the murder, or that somehow
Banquo's descendants and not his own
would one day reign, just as the witches had
foretold.

"To be thus is nothing, but to be safely thus," he muttered to himself. "Our fears in Banquo stick deep."

Macbeth decided that the only way he could hold on to his crown and pass it on to

his own children was to murder Banquo and his son, Fleance. To this end he invited all the local thanes to a feast. As Banquo and Fleance made their way to the palace, they were brutally attacked by Macbeth's hired assassins. Fleance managed to escape, but Banquo died.

"O, treachery! Fly, good Fleance, fly, fly, fly!" cried Banquo as he lay dying. "Thou mayst revenge."

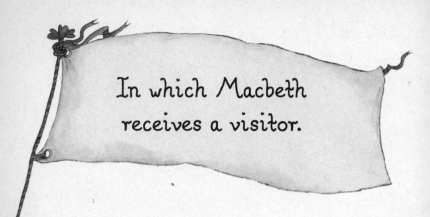

In which Macbeth
receives a visitor.

Oblivious to this horrific deed, the other

thanes were merrily dining with King

Macbeth and his queen. Macbeth was

tense and
nervous,
but tried to
put aside
his guilt.
Then, just as

he stood to give a toast, Banquo's bloody, wounded ghost appeared and silently sat down in Macbeth's seat.

"Which of you have done this?" asked Macbeth in horror.

But neither the thanes nor the queen could understand what he meant, as they could not see Banquo.

"Thou canst not say I did it," shouted Macbeth at the spectre. "Never shake thy gory locks at me."

There was an uncomfortable shuffling amongst the thanes and some made to leave.

"Why do you make such faces?" whispered his wife. "When all's done, you look but on a stool."

Macbeth was so unnerved by the ghost and the wounds it bore, which had been inflicted by his own henchmen, that the queen finally dismissed their guests, pretending that the king was sometimes afflicted by strange visions.

In which further
prophecies are revealed.

From then on, both Macbeth and his queen
began to suffer long, sleepless nights, filled
with hideous dreams. Macbeth's wife, who
had been so bold and ruthless, began to feel
that she would never wash the blood of guilt
from her hands. Yet both were still obsessed
with keeping the throne. Macbeth decided to
return to the heath to seek out the witches
and ask them what the future held.

Macbeth set out across the heath on another night of thundering skies. He finally found the three witches in a cave, chanting over a cauldron of boiling hell-broth.

"Round about the cauldron go; in the poison'd entrails throw. Double, double toil and trouble; fire burn and cauldron bubble," they cried.

As Macbeth stood watching, three apparitions rose from the cauldron: the first was an armed head which warned Macbeth to beware of Macduff, the Thane of Fife; the second was a bloody child who told Macbeth that no man born of woman could harm him; the third was another child, wearing a crown and holding a tree, who reassured Macbeth that he would never be vanquished until

Great Birnam Wood came to Dunsinane Hill, where Macbeth's castle stood.

When Macbeth asked if Banquo's heirs would reign, the cauldron sank into the ground and eight ghostly kings passed by, followed by Banquo's ghost. The last king carried a mirror which showed many more

kings, and Macbeth knew that they were Banquo's descendants. It was as he had feared – Banquo's son Fleance had escaped.

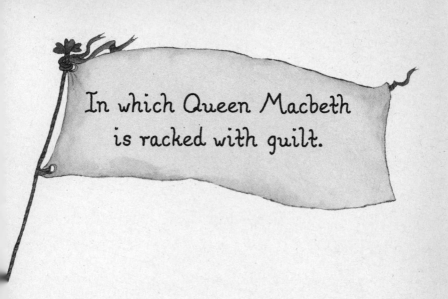

In which Queen Macbeth
is racked with guilt.

Macbeth's visit to the witches had done
nothing to make him feel that his crown was
safe. If anything, he felt more insecure than
ever. So when he heard that Macduff had
gone to England to join forces against him
with Prince Malcolm, Macbeth ordered the
death of Macduff's wife and children.

A messenger carried this terrible news
to Macduff in England. He was stunned.

He heard the words but could hardly believe
the horror of such a deed.

"All my pretty ones? Did you say all?"
he cried. "What, all my pretty chickens
and their dam at one fell swoop?" Nothing
would ever wipe out the desolation of such
a loss.

"Let's make us medicines of our great
revenge, to cure this deadly grief," said
Malcolm. Now they were more determined
than ever to reclaim the crown from such an
unworthy king.

This terrible murder of innocent children and their mother lost Macbeth many friends. He and his wife began to feel increasingly isolated, and their guilt grew. Though Queen Macbeth, as she now was, had the crown she had longed for, her life had become a living nightmare. She wandered the castle trying to wash away the blood of King Duncan from her hands and clothes – blood that had long gone, but blood that haunted her still. "Out, damned spot! Out I say!" she would cry.

After days and nights of the queen not sleeping or eating, her servant called the court doctor. But he had no medicines to ease a guilty mind.

"Here's the smell of the blood still," cried the queen as the doctor and waiting woman looked on helplessly. "All the perfumes of Arabia will not sweeten this little hand. Oh, oh, oh!"

Eventually, Lady Macbeth was unable to bear the ghastly visions any more, and she died. Macbeth now felt more hated and alone than ever. His wife had been his guiding force, his partner in crime. "She should have died hereafter," he groaned. "There would have been time for such a word."

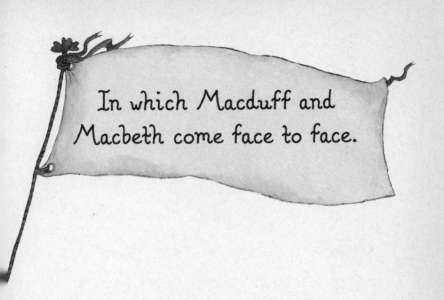

In which Macduff and Macbeth come face to face.

Macbeth was still reeling from his wife's death when a soldier who had been on watch approached him.

"I should report that which I say I saw, but know not how to do it," he said nervously.

"Well, say, sir," cried Macbeth impatiently.

"I look'd towards Birnam, and anon, methought, the wood began to move."

"Liar and slave!" cried Macbeth furiously.

But the watch was not a liar, for thousands of Prince Malcolm's troops were fast approaching, shielded behind branches cut from Great Birnam Wood. Thus it appeared that the wood moved towards Dunsinane Hill and Macbeth's castle – the event the witches said would precede Macbeth's downfall.

Macbeth still believed himself

invulnerable – even if Great Birnam Wood appeared to be moving towards his castle, he knew he would never be killed in battle.

Hadn't the witches said that no man of woman born would ever kill him? So, gathering his courage, he rallied his remaining forces and waged a bloody war against Malcolm's forces, until Macduff spotted him.

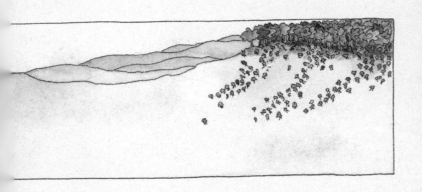

"Turn, hell-hound, turn!" cried Macduff, his sword held high.

Macbeth turned and as their swords clashed, Macbeth cried out, "Let fall thy blade on vulnerable crests; I bear a charmed life, which must not yield to one of woman born."

"Despair thy charm," cried Macduff in triumph. "Macduff was from his mother's womb untimely ripp'd!"

Macbeth's sword slackened in his hand. Macduff had not been born by natural means – he had been taken from his mother's womb by surgeons. Macbeth knew that this meant his end had come.

Macduff, with all the pain of his lost family in his sword, made sure his enemy's death was swift and bloody. With one sword stroke, he parted Macbeth's head from his body and then carried it to Prince Malcolm,

the rightful heir to King Duncan's throne.

"Hail, king! For so thou art!" cried

Macduff, triumphantly. "Hail, King of

Scotland!"

So Prince Malcolm claimed back his

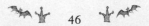

father's throne and the Scottish people
rejoiced. The wicked reign of Macbeth and
his ambitious wife had ended, just as had
been prophesied. Scotland was at peace,
ruled once more by a true and noble king.

WILLIAM SHAKESPEARE was a popular playwright, poet and actor who lived in Elizabethan England. He married in Stratford-upon-Avon aged eighteen and had three children, although one died in childhood. Shakespeare then moved to London, where he wrote 39 plays and over 150 sonnets, many of which are still very popular today. In fact, his plays are performed more often than those of any other playwright, and he died 450 years ago! His gravestone includes a curse against interfering with his burial place, possibly to deter people from opening it in search of unpublished manuscripts. It reads, "Blessed be the man that spares these stones, and cursed be he that moves my bones." Spooky!

MARCIA WILLIAMS' mother was a novelist and her father a playwright, so it's not surprising that Marcia ended up an author herself. Although she never trained formally as an artist, she found that motherhood, and the time she spent later as a nursery school teacher, inspired her to start writing and illustrating children's books.

Marcia's books bring to life some of the world's all-time favourite stories and some colourful historical characters. Her hilarious retellings and clever observations will have children laughing out loud and coming back for more!